JACKIE and thE SHADOW SNATCHER

JACKIE and the SHADOW SNATCHER
by LARRY DI FIORI

ALFRED A. KNOPF · NEW YORK

FOR MY SON, LARSON

THIS IS A BORZOI BOOK PUBLISHED BY ALFRED A. KNOPF

Published in the United States by Alfred A. Knopf, an imprint of Random House Children's Books, a division of Random House, Inc., New York.

KNOPF, BORZOI BOOKS, and the colophon are registered trademarks of Random House, Inc.

www.randomhouse.com/kids

Educators and librarians, for a variety of teaching tools, visit us at www.randomhouse.com/teachers

Library of Congress Cataloging-in-Publication Data
Di Fiori, Lawrence.
Jackie and the Shadow Snatcher / Lawrence Di Fiori. — 1st ed.
p. cm.
SUMMARY: To retrieve his lost shadow, a brave little boy makes his way to the hideout of an infamous criminal.
ISBN 0-375-87515-8 (trade) — ISBN 0-375-97515-2 (lib. bdg.)
[1. Shadows—Fiction. 2. Lost and found possessions—Fiction.] I. Title.
PZ7.D542Jac 2006 [E]—dc22
2005018290

MANUFACTURED IN CHINA
10 9 8 7 6 5 4 3 2 1
First Edition